How A Unicorn Made Me Stop Worrying
My Unicorn Books - Volume 2
Written by Steve Herman

Copyright © 2019 by Digital Golden Solutions LLC.
Published by DG Books Publishing, an imprint of
Digital Golden Solutions LLC.

All rights reserved. No part of this publication may be reproduced, distributed, or transmitted in any form or by any means, including photocopying, recording, or other electronic or mechanical methods, without the prior written permission of the publisher, except in the case of brief quotations embodied in critical reviews and certain other noncommercial uses permitted by copyright law.

Information contained within this book is for entertainment and educational purposes only. Although the author and publisher have made every effort to ensure that the information in this book was correct at press time, the author and publisher do not assume and hereby disclaim any liability to any party for any loss, damage, or disruption caused by errors or omissions, whether such errors or omissions result from negligence, accident, or any other cause.

ISBN: 978-1-950280-10-0 (paperback)
ISBN: 978-1-950280-11-7 (hardcover)

www.MyUnicornBooks.com

First Edition: August 2019
10 9 8 7 6 5 4 3 2 1

I'm so pleased to meet you! I'm Allyson Ann McNally,
But that's a lot of name to say, so folks just call me "Allie."
I even have some nicknames – I'm known as "Allie Cat."
When I mess up, I'm "Allie Oops!" What do you think of that?!

Guess what! I have a *unicorn* – Yes! You heard that right! –
The best friend I have ever had, her name is *Dazzle Delight*.
Dazzle has a nickname, too. I call her "Dazzle D,"
And everywhere I go, you can bet she goes with me.

We start each day with breakfast. We both like eggs and ham,
But she likes glitter on her toast, while I prefer grape jam.

Rainbows spring from Dazzle's horn,
we hop on and slide right down,
And land atop a cotton cloud high up above the town.

And as everybody knows, a unicorn can fly;
When I ride upon her back, I get to touch the sky!

I taste a golden sunbeam; the raindrops kiss my skin;
We race across the meadow – She always lets me win!

One day I didn't want to play; she saw that I was down;
"What can I do to help," she asked,
"to turn your frown around?"

"Doctor says that I might need glasses," I said to Dazzle D.
"What if the other kids at school start making fun of me?

"And at recess on the playground, I saw my buddy, Bart,
Playing tag with someone else; it almost broke my heart!"

"What if he has a new best friend?
Who will I play with now?
Will I need to make new friends?
I'm not sure that I know how!"

"This weekend, there's a birthday party; I have been invited,
But I don't want to go; I'm not feeling too excited."

"What if I do not know the other children who are there? There'll be no one to play with, and that I just can't bear!"

"I have a brand new mermaid toy; What if my brother, Ben, Takes my doll away from me, and I get mad and then..."

"I yell at him and make him cry – It's happened once or twice,
But I was the one who got in trouble for not acting very nice!"

Dazzle Delight was ready, and she knew just what to say
To put a smile upon my face and chase my blues away.
"Allie Ann, you've got this! There's no need for you to fret
Or waste your time with worry; you shouldn't be upset."

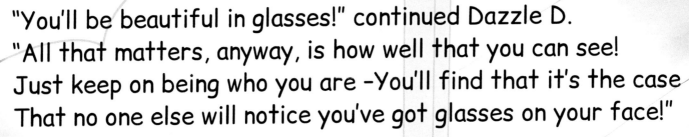

"You'll be beautiful in glasses!" continued Dazzle D.
"All that matters, anyway, is how well that you can see!
Just keep on being who you are –You'll find that it's the case
That no one else will notice you've got glasses on your face!"

"And don't worry that your buddy, Bart,
has made another friend.
That shouldn't even bother you;
in fact, I recommend
That a person have a lot of pals,
and rest assured it's true.
Your friend can play with someone else
and still be friends with you."

"And about that birthday party, I think that you should go!
It's a chance to make new friends, and Allie, even though
You may be kind of bashful, that's not a reason why
You should miss this opportunity – Allie, don't be shy!"

"Don't worry that your brother, Ben,
might take your doll away;
He might not even want to play with mermaids, anyway!"

"But if he wants to play with it, you really ought to share. When he's done, he'll give it back, so Allie, don't despair."

"And when you're playing softball;
you shouldn't be distressed.
It doesn't matter if you win;
have fun and play your best"

"Your team will not be mad at you; in fact, they'll understand Sometimes people make mistakes, and things don't go as planned."

"And when you can't go camping, I know just how you feel,
But trust me, Allie, when I say, it's really no big deal.
Read a book, bake a cake, then look up; you just might see
A rainbow slide up in the sky! What fun!" said Dazzle D.

So Dazzle Delight taught me not to worry or feel blue -
I hope you paid attention, and you learned the lesson, too.

Life is filled with "*What if?*" moments,
but know that there's no need
To think about what might go wrong –
Believe that you'll succeed!

Get your FREE Gift from Dazzle at
www.MyUnicornBooks.com/gift

READ MORE ABOUT ALLIE AND DAZZLE!

My Unicorn Books - Volume 1

My Unicorn Books - Volume 2

VISIT
WWW.MYUNICORNBOOKS.COM

Made in the USA
San Bernardino, CA
23 December 2019

62330910R00024